Don't Get Lost!

By Pat Hutchins

 Greenwillow Books, *An Imprint of* HarperCollins*Publishers*

Don't Get Lost!
Copyright © 2004 by Pat Hutchins
All rights reserved. Manufactured in China by South China Printing Company Ltd.
www.harperchildrens.com

Pen and ink and felt-tipped markers were used to prepare the full-color art.
The text type is Quorum Book.

Library of Congress Cataloging-in-Publication Data

Hutchins, Pat, (date).
Don't get lost! / by Pat Hutchins.
p. cm.
"Greenwillow Books."
Summary: When Little Piglet, Little Lamb, Little Calf,
and Little Foal take a walk across the fields after breakfast,
they seem to lose their way as they try to head for home.
ISBN 0-06-055996-9 (trade). ISBN 0-06-055997-7 (lib. bdg.)
[1. Lost children—Fiction. 2. Domestic animals—Fiction.]
I. Title: Do not get lost. II. Title.
PZ7.H96165Dm 2004 [E]—dc22 2003013810

First Edition 10 9 8 7 6 5 4 3 2 1

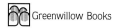 Greenwillow Books

For Aidan

Little Piglet had just finished his breakfast.
"Can I go for a walk across the fields?"
he asked his mother.
"Yes," said his mother, "but don't get lost,
and be back in time for dinner!"

Little Piglet passed Little Lamb and her mother.

Little Lamb had just finished her breakfast as well.

"I'm going for a walk across the fields,"
said Little Piglet.

"Can I go with Piglet?" asked Little Lamb.

"Yes," said her mother, "but don't get lost,
and be back in time for dinner!"

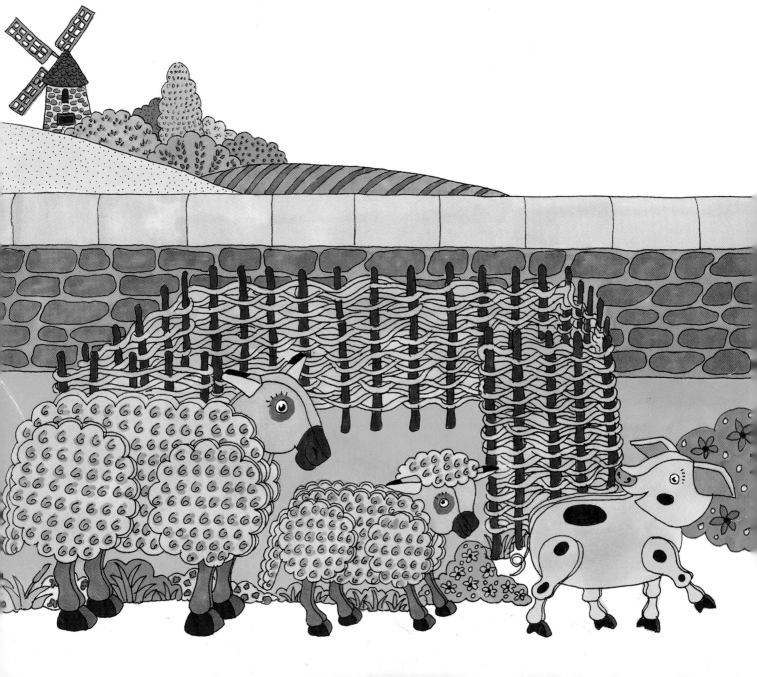

Little Piglet and Little Lamb passed Little Calf
and her mother, and Little Foal and his mother.

"We're going for a walk across the fields,"
said Little Piglet and Little Lamb.
"Can we go with Piglet and Lamb?"
Little Calf and Little Foal asked their mothers.
"Yes," said their mothers, "but don't get lost,
and be back in time for dinner!"

So Little Piglet and Little Lamb
and Little Calf and Little Foal
went out of the farmyard
and into the fields.

They went into a field with an apple tree in it.

Big ripe red apples hung from the branches.

Little Piglet loved apples,

but he didn't eat any

because he'd just had his breakfast.

So . . . Little Piglet, Little Lamb,
Little Calf, and Little Foal
chased one another round and round
the tree until they felt dizzy,
and when they'd had enough of that,

they went into the next field,

which had bales of sweet hay stacked in it.

Little Calf and Little Foal loved hay,

but they didn't eat any

because they'd just had their breakfast.

So . . . Little Piglet, Little Lamb,

Little Calf, and Little Foal

played hide-and-seek

among the bales until they were covered in hay,

and when they'd had enough of that,

they went into the next field,

which had rows of freshly dug juicy turnips in it.

Little Lamb loved turnips

but she didn't eat any

because she'd just had her breakfast.

So . . . Little Piglet, Little Lamb,
Little Calf, and Little Foal
raced up and down
the rows of turnips
until their legs ached,
and when they'd had enough of that,

they went into the next field,
and splashed in the pond
until they were soaking wet.

Then Little Piglet said,
"I'm hungry! It must be time for dinner!"

Little Lamb and Little Calf and Little Foal
said, "So are we! We're very hungry!"
So they set off for home.
"We could eat some turnips on the way home,"
said Little Lamb. "I love turnips!"

But when they went into the next field,
there weren't any turnips.

"We could eat some hay on the way back,"
said Little Calf and Little Foal.
"We love hay!"

But when they went into the next field,
there wasn't any hay.

"We could eat some apples on the way back,"
said Little Piglet.
"I love apples!"

But when they went into the next field,
there weren't any apples.
"Oh, dear!" said Little Lamb and Little Calf
and Little Foal.
"We should have come through
a field with turnips in it,
and a field with hay in it,
and a field with apples in it.
We must have come the wrong way!"

And they all felt very frightened
and very hungry
and very lost.

But then Little Piglet saw the farmyard.

And waiting for them were Little Calf's mother,
Little Foal's mother, Little Lamb's mother,
and Little Piglet's mother.

"We're glad you're back in time for dinner,"
they all said.
"We've got freshly dug juicy turnips,"
said Little Lamb's mother.

"And sweet new hay," said Little Calf's mother
and Little Foal's mother.
"And big ripe red apples,"
said Little Piglet's mother.

"And we're glad you didn't get lost!"